KU-496-358

ELIZABETH LINDSAY

Magic Pony

5. Ghost in the House

Illustrated by John Eastwood

Hippo

For Kiran

221O5388T

CLACKMANNANSHIRE
4.99 LIBRARIES F

Scholastic Children's Books,
Commonwealth House, 1-19 New Oxford Street,
London WC1A 1NU, UK
a division of Scholastic Ltd
London ~ New York ~ Toronto ~ Sydney ~ Auckland

Published in the UK by Scholastic Ltd, 1998

Text copyright © Elizabeth Lindsay, 1998
Illustrations copyright © John Eastwood, 1998

ISBN 0 590 19891 2

Printed by Cox & Wyman Ltd, Reading, Berks.

2 4 6 8 10 9 7 5 3 1

All rights reserved

The rights of Elizabeth Lindsay and John Eastwood to be identified respectively
as the author and illustrator of this work have been asserted by them in
accordance with the Copyright, Designs and Patents Act, 1988.

This book is sold subject to the condition that it shall not, by way of trade or
otherwise, be lent, resold, hired out, or otherwise circulated without the
publisher's prior consent in any form of binding or cover other than that in
which it is published and without a similar condition, including this condition,
being imposed upon the subsequent purchaser.

Chapter 1

Penelope is Poorly

Natty was in the kitchen, pulling at the ring on a sardine tin in order to give Tabitha her special Saturday pussy-cat breakfast. This morning the toaster had refused to work and, before staggering outside with a pile of washing to peg out, Mum had explained that you can leave a toaster to get on with it but bread under a grill needs watching. On the grill-pan four slices of well-browned toast were darkening to a point beyond done. The sardine smell had Tabitha winding herself eagerly around Natty's legs purring loudly, and the smell of burning toast had Natty diving to the rescue.

There was a knock at the front door.

"Somebody at the door!" Dad shouted from the living-room, unscrewing another tiny part from the broken toaster. In her panic to save the toast Natty didn't hear – she was too busy switching off the grill and blowing on the charcoaled pieces.

"Miaow," said Tabitha as a reminder.

"Coming."

Natty put down the grill-pan, grabbed a fork and dug out the sardines. Tabitha stretched up and, shoving her nose into the bowl as soon as she could, tucked in.

There was another, louder knock.

"Somebody please answer the door," shouted Dad. Jamie's footsteps clattered down the stairs and clumped across the hall. "Thank goodness someone's going." Another screw joined the collection on a plate.

"I've burnt the toast."

"I know. I can smell it." The hall door opened and Jamie came in. "Who is it?" Dad asked.

"Mr Potter! He didn't stop. He asked me to give this letter to Natty." Jamie held out a pink envelope.

"What letter?" asked Natty, darting to look.

In typical brotherly fashion Jamie sent the letter spinning across the room. Too curious to complain, Natty caught it.

"And I know what's in it and I told Mr Potter you would," said Jamie.

Natty looked at the envelope. Her name was printed in bold black letters and underlined. "Penelope's typed it on her new computer."

"Well, aren't you going to open it?"

"I am," said Natty, skipping across the room. "Upstairs."

"What about the toast?" cried Dad.

"Jamie can do it."

"That's not fair," objected Jamie. But he was too late. Natty was gone.

Once in her bedroom, Natty pushed the door closed and sat on her bed. Then she looked up at the pony poster above her chest of drawers. The head of a handsome chestnut pony stared down at her.

"Ned," said Natty. "This is a letter from Penelope Potter. Why do you think she's writing to me?" Natty waited, hoping for a reply, but none came. The pony in the poster remained a picture.

"Please magic, please work today," wished Natty. "Make Ned come alive." Natty jumped from the bed. Her three china ponies, Esmerelda, Prince, and Percy were looking out of the window. She looked out too. But this morning the field across the lane was empty.

Natty tore open the envelope and pulled out a pink sheet of paper.

"It's even got a pony logo," she said. "I'll read it to you, shall I? Then maybe you'll come alive. We could have an amazing magic pony adventure all day if you did." She looked longingly up at Ned, remembering her first glimpse of him in the window of Cosby's Magic Emporium, the shop where Jamie bought his magic tricks. Had Mr Cosby known all along that Ned's poster was magic, that the pony in the picture came alive, and that sometimes he might be proper pony size and sometimes as tiny as Percy, the smallest of her china horses? Natty was sure that no other pony poster in the whole world was so special or such a secret. She smoothed out the letter and cleared her throat.

Dear Natty,

I was sick in the night and now I feel yukky. Today I was going to a horse show but Mummy says I am to rest. Pebbles is in his stable. He needs feeding (half a scoopful of pony nuts) and turning out (headcollar in tack room). Then his stable needs mucking out. Tell my dad if you can't and he'll have to do it. But I know I can rely on you.

From a poorly friend,

Penelope Potter

PS When you've finished come straight to the house and tell me how Pebbles is.

"Oh, yes," cried Natty, flinging her window wide. By leaning out she could just see into Penelope's little stable-yard. There was Pebbles, head out over his stable door, waiting for his breakfast. "I must go at once. See you later, Ned."

Then, not bothering to close the window, Natty raced for the door. The pony in the poster turned ever so slightly to watch her go.

Downstairs, Natty burst into the living-room.

"I'm going to look after Pebbles," she informed everyone.

"I knew she would," said Jamie.

"Not before breakfast," said Dad, lifting the plate with all the toaster bits and putting it on top of the television.

"There is no breakfast," said Natty. "I burnt it."

"And I've made some more," called Mum from the kitchen. "Toast is on its way. Put on your wellies if you're going to muck out. I don't want dung all over your trainers. You can take your toast with you if you're in such a rush."

"Thanks, Mum," said Natty, running into the kitchen to find her boots.

"What do you want on it?"

"Honey, please." Natty pulled off her trainers and crammed her feet into her wellingtons. She took the offered toast.

"Here," said Mum. "You can give Pebbles these with my compliments." And she handed Natty a paper bag. Natty shook it. "Carrot fingers," explained Mum. "Nice long ones so he won't choke. You can add them to his pony nuts. And give Penelope my love when you go and see her. Tell her I hope she gets better soon."

"I will," said Natty, and with the toast between her teeth, she flung open the back door, hurried across the grass and round the house to the side gate.

Chapter 2

Looking After Pebbles

Once in the lane, Natty set off purposefully towards Penelope's stable-yard. This was the first time she had ever looked after Pebbles all by herself and she was really excited. It made up for her disappointment that Ned's magic was not working today. She chewed her toast, hardly noticing she was eating.

By the time she reached the stable-yard gate there was only the crust left. She held it between her teeth while she undid the latch.

A long, low whicker came from Pebbles's stable.

"I know, I know, you're saying where's my breakfast." Natty held out her hand, fingers flat, balancing the toast crust.

Pebbles's lips wobbled open and the crust was gone. He crunched happily while Natty stroked his dappled grey neck and looked in the stable. "Not a wisp of hay left. No wonder you're hungry." Smelling the carrots, Pebbles pushed at the paper bag. "No! You can have the carrots with your breakfast. I'll get it now."

Natty ran to the tack room and opened the door. She was greeted by the inviting smell of leather, saddle-soap and pony. Lifting the lid of the feed bin she measured half a scoopful of pony nuts into a bucket and shook the carrot fingers on top.

Back outside another long, low whicker greeted her, and Pebbles, with ears pricked, stretched his neck towards his breakfast. Natty held the bucket behind her as she undid the stable door.

"Back, Pebbles," she commanded and the pony stepped politely out of the way. But the moment she put down the bucket, his head was in it. Natty shut the door and smiled. "Breakfast at last, eh boy?"

"Yoo hoo, Natty!"

Natty turned to find Mrs Plumley, their neighbour from next door, beaming at her from the gate, and Ruddles, Mrs Plumley's dog, wagging his tail.

"Hello, Mrs Plumley," said Natty, skipping over. "Hello, Ruddles." Natty bent down as the little dog pulled against his lead to say hello. She gave him a big cuddle and Ruddles gave her a big lick.

"Oh, help," she cried. "Right on the nose."

"He don't mind noses, Natty," chuckled Mrs Plumley. "He gives all his friends big doggy kisses, don't you Ruddles?"

"Woof, woof," barked Ruddles in agreement.

"Now where's young Penelope this morning? Her mum told me she was off to a horse show today."

"Not very well," said Natty. "So I'm looking after Pebbles."

"Oh dear, I'm sorry she's poorly," said Mrs Plumley. "Well, when you see her, you tell her from me to get better soon. And that I'm glad to see she's got a friend for Pebbles at last."

"What sort of a friend?"

"A pony friend, of course. I knew by the chestnut colour it wasn't Pebbles. Now that's nice, I thought."

Natty's heart skipped a beat and she hoped that, just maybe, Ned's magic was working and he'd come out of his picture. She raced across the yard to look. She even climbed to the top of the gate to make herself higher but there was no pony in Pebbles's field.

"There isn't a pony there," said Natty, trying not to sound disappointed.

"Well now, I could have sworn I saw one grazing over by Penelope's blue barrel jumps," Mrs Plumley said. "But there you are, dear. It's my eyes playing tricks again. And truth is, I wasn't wearing my glasses. Come along Ruddles, we must leave Natty to get on. We're off to do our shopping."

"Bye, Mrs Plumley."

"Bye bye, Natty dear. Call in and see us soon."

With a wave, Mrs Plumley and Ruddles continued on down the lane towards the main road. Natty longed to groom Pebbles's dappled coat but the pony was looking expectantly from his stable and she knew he wanted to go into his field. Natty ran to the tack room and, putting the hoof-pick in her pocket, grabbed the headcollar. Back in the stable she slipped the headcollar on and tied Pebbles to the string on the tying-up ring. Then carefully lifting each foot, she picked out the dirt with the hoof-pick.

"There," she said. "All done." Untying the halter rope she led Pebbles out of his stable and across the yard to the field gate. Once he was free Pebbles bucked four times and cantered off. Natty admired his mane and tail streaming in the breeze before carefully fastening the gate. Now she had the stable to clean.

Penelope often let her muck out, so she knew the routine. She collected the pitchfork and wheelbarrow then got started. By the time she wheeled the full barrow to the dung-heap, Pebbles was grazing quietly. To her disappointment there was no sign of a chestnut pony grazing with him. Mrs Plumley's eyes certainly had been deceiving her.

Natty swept the yard, rinsed out Pebbles's food bucket then put away the broom, wheelbarrow and pitchfork.

By the time Mr Potter drove down the drive from Penelope's house, across the lane and into the yard, everything was neat and tidy.

"Thanks for doing all that," he said from the car. "Penelope says go and see her. I've just fetched Trudi. So between the pair of you you should manage to cheer her up, poor lamb. She's upset about missing her showjumping."

"Who wouldn't be," sighed Natty to herself, wishing she could do showjumping too. To Mr Potter she said, "All right. I'll go and see her now."

"That's my girl," said Mr Potter. "Now Penelope and Trudi want Wally Whizzer Wonderstick Ice-Creams. What would you like?"

"Me?" said Natty, surprised to be asked. "I'll have the same, please."

"As I've got to drive all the way to the supermarket I'll get a boxful."

"A boxful," gasped Natty as Mr Potter reversed out of the yard and drove off towards the main road. Natty only had a Wally Whizzer Wonderstick Ice-Cream on very special occasions. Maybe this was turning into one?

Trudi was Penelope's best friend and if she was at the house Penelope must be feeling better. I just hope they don't gang up on me like they do on the school bus, Natty thought.

She admired Pebbles's clean and tidy straw bed, his fresh bucket of water and bursting haynet for the last time and closed the stable door. Perhaps this afternoon Penelope might be well enough to take Pebbles for a ride and would let her do some grooming after all. She hung up the headcollar and hoof-pick in the tack room and cast an eye round the little stable-yard.

"Extremely neat and tidy, Natty. Well done!" The unexpected voice made Natty jump and she spun round. To her astonishment a chestnut pony leaned out over Pebbles's stable door. "The only problem is you've locked me in."

"Ned," cried Natty. "Ned!" And she rushed to fling her arms around the chestnut pony's neck. "I didn't think the magic would happen today."

"Well it did and here I am," said the pony. "Please will you let me out?" Natty undid the bolt and opened the door. Ned pranced into the yard. "I see Penelope's got you busy as usual. Brushing and sweeping and so on. You've certainly done a good job."

"Penelope's poorly."

"I know," said Ned. "You told me. And as you're on your way to visit her, I'll come too."

"But what if somebody sees you?"

"Leave me to bother about that." He gave Natty a gentle nudge with his nose.

"After all, you didn't see me go into the stable, did you now?"

"You must have been your tiny self, that's why. But Mrs Plumley saw you in the field."

"True. I was a little careless, but it was good to get a few mouthfuls of fresh grass."

"Well please don't be careless again," cautioned Natty.

"There's no need to worry about me. Just lead the way to Penelope."

Chapter 3

Three's a Crowd

Natty pushed away all her anxieties. It was good to have Ned walking at her side as she crossed the lane from the stable-yard into Penelope's back drive. Natty's wellies and four pony feet crunched along the gravel until they came into the courtyard.

"Once upon a time, long ago, these

garages were stables," said Natty, pointing to three garage doors. "Just imagine having horses in your back garden."

"Well," said Ned. "I don't think that's as good as having one in your bedroom."

"I was forgetting that," laughed Natty. She became suddenly serious. "I can't knock on the door until you are your tiny self, Ned. If Mrs Potter sees you, she'll be furious. Ponies aren't allowed in the garden."

But Natty didn't have a chance to knock. There were two impatient barks from inside the house and the back door opened. She jumped in front of Ned and stretched her arms wide as if by doing so she could blot him from view and riveted her gaze to the face that looked down at her. It was Mrs Potter, clutching a fluffy, coffee-coloured poodle.

"There you are at last, Natty," she said, and gazing down at Natty's startled face asked, "What's the matter?"

"I, er…!" Natty glanced over her shoulder. Ned had vanished. "Nothing." She lowered her arms sheepishly. "I didn't know you had a dog."

"I don't. Penelope's looking after Pom Pom for her Aunt Diana."

"He's very pretty."

"I suppose he is if you like dogs," sniffed Mrs Potter. "Take your wellingtons off and leave them on the newspaper by the washing-machine. Penelope and Trudi are in the television-room. They're expecting you. As Penelope's ill I'm taking Pom Pom out for his walk."

Natty obediently pulled off her wellies and stepped into the utility room. The door to the kitchen was open. After her house, Penelope's house was like a palace, the rooms were so big. She plonked her wellies on the first convenient piece of newspaper.

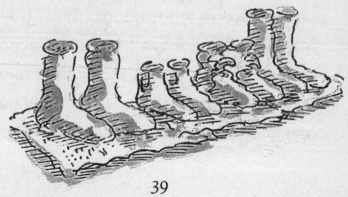

"Goodbye," said Mrs Potter and she pulled the back door closed behind her, just missing the tiny chestnut pony galloping across the doormat on its way to the kitchen.

"Ned," whispered Natty. "Wait for me." Natty skidded across the slippery floor tiles, past a cooker, a fridge, a freezer and a row of gleaming kitchen gadgets. As ponies weren't allowed in the garden Natty wondered what Mrs Potter would do if she knew she had one in the house. She glanced under the table but Ned had completely disappeared.

She peeped round the door into the hall and was met by a strong lavender smell, even though the flower vase on the hall table was empty. Polish, Natty guessed. The wooden floor shone and dotted here and there like giant stepping stones were an array of rectangular rugs.

Natty resisted the temptation to go skating on her socks and tiptoed to what she thought was the television-room door. As she hardly ever came into Penelope's house she hoped she'd remembered it correctly.

She took a quick look round, wondering where Ned could have got to, before pushing the door open. The room was in semi-darkness but she could make out the television and the heavy curtains draping the windows. Leaving the door ajar she went inside and her toes met the softness of a thick pile carpet. She expected Penelope to be lying down but tiptoeing forward she could see that the sofa in front of the television was empty. The door slammed.

"Whoo, whooo whooooo!" A wailing voice was behind her. Before she could

turn she was enveloped by a great cloth.
Hands grasped and twirled her and she
could do nothing but spin. Stumbling,
she tripped and was pushed on to the
sofa, banging her elbow. First one lot of
shrieks and then another lot closed in,
and wriggling fingers tickled her.

"We are the ghosts of the house!" Penelope was instantly recognizable.

"Get off," Natty shouted.

"We have come to haunt you-oooooooo!" Trudi's unmistakable high-pitched tones joined in. Natty wriggled away in a fury and rolled across the floor.

Struggling to free herself, she managed to pull off what turned out to be a bedspread, and sat in front of the television, nursing her aching arm, her face a furious pink.

"No need to look so cross," said Penelope. "We wanted to give you a surprise, that's all."

"A very little fright," said Trudi, with one of her pretend smiles. "We got the idea from the ghost video we were watching."

"And now we'll pull the curtains," said Penelope. "Can you do it, Trude – I feel all weak and wobbly."

Still seething, Natty struggled to her feet, but she wasn't going to give them the pleasure of seeing how upset she was. Secretly she rubbed her elbow.

"I just came to tell you about Pebbles," she said. "I thought you were ill?"

"I am," said Penelope, flopping back on to a pile of cushions. "Too ill to go out, too ill to do anything much." Trudi swished open the tall curtains and a stream of sunlight flooded the room. "Not that wide," said Penelope. "We'll never be able to see the video with that much light." She turned wide-eyed towards Natty and put on a trembly voice. "We're watching *Hullabaloo and the Haunting of Flintstone Castle*. Really spooky."

"I'm not stopping to see that," said Natty, realizing that as usual they were ganging up on her. "I've got things to do."

Before she could reach the door Trudi beat her to it and stood, barring the way, with an oily grin on her face.

"But you haven't told Penelope anything about Pebbles. How does she know you've looked after him properly?"

"If she doesn't believe I have, she can check for herself," said Natty, refusing to be intimidated.

"Oh, Natty, don't go," said Penelope. "I do want to know how Pebbles is. Please come and tell me. And Daddy's fetching you a Wally Whizzer Wonderstick. You can't go until you've had that." Natty sighed. She had to admit she was tempted by the Wally Whizzer.

"Oh, all right. But no playing about." She sat next to Penelope.

"So how is Pebbles?"

"Yes, how is Pebbles?" repeated Trudi, leaning over the back of the sofa and staring straight into Natty's face.

"Did you give him his breakfast?" Penelope asked.

"Yes, did you give him his breakfast?" repeated Trudi. Then with a sudden lunge Penelope pulled out a can from behind a cushion and Trudi one from behind her back. They took aim and fired. Natty jumped out of the way, but too late to stop herself being showered in Rainbow Sticky Foam.

"You're hateful, both of you!" she cried. "This stuff takes for ever to get off."

"Now now, Natty," said Penelope, falling on to her cushions and shaking with laughter. "Can't you take a joke?"

"No sense of humour," said Trudi, flouncing round the sofa to sit beside her friend. "I can't think why you asked her to look after Pebbles. He deserves someone much nicer than her."

"Don't be mean, Trudi," said Penelope. "Natty's at her best when mucking out and that sort of thing. She's very good at wheelbarrowing the pongy bits."

"I wondered what was so whiffy," said Trudi. "Pooh!" And she clasped her nose for dramatic effect.

Natty bit her lip and ignored them, deciding the best way to get rid of the Rainbow Sticky Foam was to give herself a shake.

"No!" cried Penelope. "Now it's all over the carpet. Mummy will go mad."

"Better get Natty to hoover it up," said Trudi.

"No chance!"

"You do it, Trude," said Penelope. "Doing the Sticky Foam was your idea. I want to watch the ghost video. Spooky, spooky, *spooooky*!"

Bang! Bang! Bang! Something hammered against the television-room door.

"What's that?" said Penelope.

Nobody moved. Then Trudi, giggling nervously, tiptoed across the carpet and pulled the door open. Expecting something to burst in, Penelope crouched behind the sofa arm. Trudi looked in the hall.

"That's weird," she said. "We all heard the banging, didn't we? But there's no one there!"

Chapter 4

Spooks in the House

Only Natty saw the tiny chestnut pony canter across the carpet and push his way under the fringe on the side of the sofa. Her spirits lifted; Ned had come to her rescue. She kept a wary eye on the floor, wondering what he would do next, and took a deep breath.

"Wow! Spooks on the video, spooks in

the house." She raised her eyebrows and shrugged to make her point, guessing that Ned had become his big self and done the door banging before going tiny again. She was going to enjoy this. "Old houses often do have ghosts, don't they? I bet this house is old enough to have loads."

"Don't be stupid," said Penelope, getting up to look in the hall for herself.

"It was probably Pom Pom wanting to get in."

"Your mum has taken Pom Pom out for a walk. They were just going when I arrived."

Penelope stared bleakly into the empty hall.

"It was the wind then," said Trudi.

"Wind!" said Natty, crossing to the window. "There isn't even a teensy breeze outside today. Indoor ghost-wind maybe. They can make their own wind, ghosts can. I read it in a book so it must be true."

From the corner of her eye Natty saw Ned canter out from the other end of the sofa and make for the remote control that lay on the carpet. Natty moved nearer to Penelope and Trudi to distract them if necessary. The pony reared up and brought his front feet down first on the volume button and then the play button.

The blast of sound surprised both Trudi and Penelope who clung to each other as *Hullabaloo and the Haunting of Flintstone Castle* blared unexpectedly from the television. Ned raced behind the curtains.

"Turn it off, turn it off," shrieked Trudi.

Hiding a smile, Natty picked up the remote control.

"Hey, this is a good bit," she said, watching Hullabaloo tiptoe down some dark stone stairs to a huge studded door. He turned a giant key and the door creaked open. From deep in the gloomy dungeon, chains rattled ominously. Natty pressed the off button. "A really spooky video, just like you said, Penelope."

"How did it do it? How did the TV come on by itself?"

"I told you," said Natty. "You've got a ghost in the house. And watching ghost videos has got it going. Seeing spooky friends has reminded it to get haunting."

"I don't believe in that kind of thing," said Trudi.

"Neither do I," said Penelope, but by her wide and staring eyes and the break in her voice, Natty could tell she was scared.

"What's that noise in the kitchen?" asked Natty, pretending to hear something.

Penelope looked startled. "What noise?"

"There isn't a noise," said Trudi, marching into the hall to show how brave she was. Natty nodded.

"She's probably right. Let's face it, the ghost seems to be in here."

"I'll help Trudi check the kitchen," said Penelope, scuttling after her friend.

Natty pushed the door to and turned to find the curtains billowing as if something large was suddenly behind them.

"Ned," she whispered.

The pony's head pushed between the folds while his tail swished against the wallpaper. Now there was a full-sized pony in the television room.

"Ned, they'll see you. Go tiny and let's go."

"Go!" replied Ned. "Not likely. This is just starting to be fun. Quick, Natty, get on." He burst from between the curtains, wearing his saddle and bridle.

Voices in the hall made Natty run. She charged across the room, bounced across the sofa and vaulted on to his back. As the door opened there was whirl of magic wind. Just in time, a tiny rider and tiny pony charged for the safety of the sofa fringe.

"She's gone," said Penelope.

"Good riddance," said Trudi and bounced across the sofa. "We can watch a video now."

"Not the haunting one," said Penelope. "I've gone off ghosts."

Ned trotted out from the hiding-place and Natty looked up to see Trudi's elbow lean like a fallen tree trunk over the sofa's giant side. She just had time to pull her riding hat straight before Ned set off at a canter for the hall.

"It's funny about Natty," said Penelope. "Going off like that."

"Oh, forget about her," said Trudi. "She can't take a joke – that's her trouble."

"You're right. No sense of humour."

Natty grinned, knowing she had more of a sense of humour than Penelope thought, and she stood in her stirrups while Ned cantered across the shiny floor to the bottom of the stairs.

"Hang on tight," he said. "We're going up. We've got some more haunting to do."

"But," gasped Natty, leaning into Ned's first jump, "aren't we going home?"

"Not yet," said Ned. "I think those two need a taste of their own medicine."

Natty didn't argue but concentrated on staying on. She didn't know how many stairs there were in Penelope's house, never having been up them before, and, when they arrived at the top, she was surprised by how long and wide the landing was.

"Which is Penelope's bedroom?" Ned asked.

"I don't know," whispered Natty. "What are you planning to do?"

"This," said Ned and there was a whirl of wind and to Natty's astonishment they were their big selves again. Natty felt incredibly high up and exposed, riding a pony across the landing carpet. She looked over the banisters, half expecting to see Mrs Potter in the hall, hear her gasp and pass out with the shock. Goodness, she was glad to be disguised by her magic riding clothes, in case it really happened.

"Ned, what if they see us?"

"They won't, and if they do they'll think we're ghosts. How else could a pony and rider be on the landing?"

Luckily, they didn't stay there for long; Ned wanted to find Penelope's bedroom.

"We must collect some ammunition," he said. "And then, before the haunting begins, you must go downstairs and join the others. That way they can't say it was you."

Natty dismounted and let go of the reins. Instantly her riding clothes vanished but once back in ordinary clothes, her socks were good for tiptoeing. The first room they looked into was the bathroom. Ned poked his head round the door.

"We could do something with those."

"The toilet rolls?" There were three on a stand. "What exactly?"

"You'll see. Bring them and that hat that's hanging from the tap."

"The shower cap? What do you want with that?"

"I've got an idea."

They opened another door to find a room which was probably Mr and Mrs Potter's, for inside was a gigantic bed. The next room was certainly Penelope's. On a table by the window sat the new computer, but more impressive, a whole wall was covered with a multitude of bright rosettes and pictures of Penelope, either standing with Pebbles, jumping Pebbles, trotting Pebbles, cantering Pebbles or doing a lap of honour with Pebbles, a rosette flying from his bridle.

"Look at that lot! Penelope's won loads!"

"Is that what you'd like?" Ned asked. "To win a rosette?"

"More than anything in the world," replied Natty, and then she grinned a wicked grin. "Except doing haunting." Ned wobbled his lips against a string bag full of tennis balls hanging on the back of the door. He turned to Natty.

"Well, haunting is what we will do," he said. Then he put his muzzle to her ear so he could whisper.

Chapter 5

This Ghost Rules OK!

The haunting preparations were quickly finished. Natty wore a mischievous smile as she hurried downstairs and tiptoed to the television room. She could hear the television blaring inside and, lifting her fist, she banged three times on the door. The effect was most satisfactory. Two loud squeals and two wide-eyed faces when she opened the door.

"Oh, it's you," said Penelope, with obvious relief. "We thought you'd gone home."

"No," said Natty, leaving the door open behind her. "I went to find the bathroom."

"You've been ages," said Trudi, accusingly.

"Sometimes going to the bathroom does take ages." Natty sat on the end of the sofa. "Aren't you watching the ghost video?"

"We're looking at *Dangerous Adventure* instead," said Trudi.

"Much more fun," added Penelope.

"Yes," nodded Natty. "Much better than ghosts. Hey, what was that?"

"What?" asked Penelope.

"It's that noise again." Natty grabbed

the remote control and turned down the volume. A steady clump-clumping echoed round the hall. "There, I told you. It's coming from upstairs. A sort of ghosty bumping."

Penelope eased herself up and crept to the open door. Natty and Trudi followed.

At that precise moment a red rosette fluttered from between the banister rails and landed on one of the rugs in the hall. It was followed by a green one, a yellow, a blue and a mauve.

"Rosettes," gasped Natty. "Ghost rosettes! Falling from nowhere."

"Stop it, Natty," said Penelope. "You're scaring Trudi." But Natty could see that Penelope was pretty scared herself.

"It must be the wind," said Trudi. "It must be." Knowing it was Ned – hiding round the corner tossing rosettes with his teeth – Natty worked hard to keep a straight face.

"I don't think so," she said. "The wind would blow them up, not down. Definitely a ghost dropping them, I'd say."

Bump bump bump bump.
Down the stairs
bounced a toilet
roll, unwinding
to trail a paper
streamer in its wake.

Bump bump bump bump.
Down came another one.

A third flew over
the banisters and
streamed all the
way to the front
door, like a wild
white bird.

Both girls ducked and ended up crouching on the floor. There was a long silence when nothing happened. At last Penelope stood up.

"Ha ha! Very funny, Natty. You've done all this, haven't you? That's what you were doing when you were in the bathroom. Well, I'm not rolling up all that loo roll. You can do it." And she bent to pick up a rosette.

"Don't touch it," shrieked Trudi. "Look!" She pointed to the most terrifying thing of all, a white shower cap gliding in zig-zags across the landing carpet. It turned in the most mysterious way, making one circle then another before speeding out of sight.

"I told you," Natty gasped, her expression deadly serious, for not in a million years would she let on that underneath the shower cap a tiny pony was galloping his fastest. "There *is* a ghost in the house. How could I possibly move a shower cap from down here?"

Penelope and Trudi looked at each other in terror. First one then the other ran screaming towards the kitchen door.

"Get rid of it," yelled Penelope. "Get rid of it." The big Ned quickly leaned over the banisters and lobbed a couple of tennis balls at their retreating backs, causing more screams before the door banged shut and the commotion faded into the distance.

"Hurry up, Ned," said Natty. "We've got to get out of here before they come back."

"They won't come back. They'll be hiding in the garden by now," he said. "But Mrs Potter could arrive at any moment. Quick. Come and get on."

Natty leapt over the trail of toilet roll and raced upstairs. With another vault she was astride the pony. The magic wind blew and they became a tiny pony and tiny rider, galloping for the stairs. Down they went, jump stride jump stride jump, with Natty counting steps all the way to the bottom.

Now, with miles of hall floor before them Ned raced for the kitchen door, leaping the loo-roll streamers and any rosettes in their path, galloping across a rug patterned with leaves and flowers which stretched ahead like a six-acre field. The speed was tremendous and the whistling wind brought tears to Natty's eyes.

At last the brown panels of the kitchen door loomed above them.

"I'll have to get off and open it," cried Natty.

"No, wait!" panted Ned, skidding to a halt by the skirting-board. "Someone's coming." Footsteps stopped on the other side, and the door opened. It was Mrs Potter. Ned dodged around her tree-trunk legs and sped into the kitchen.

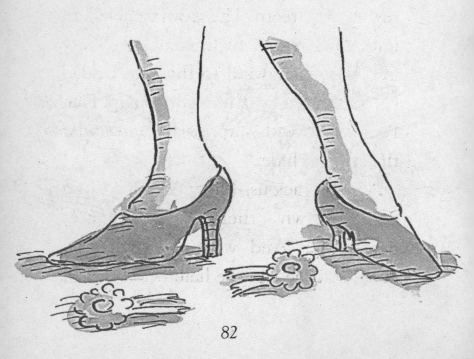

Behind them, Mrs Potter discovered the mess in the hall and gave a cry of dismay; from in front came a growl. Pom Pom bent towards them, eyes like glinting coal, his top lip curling above a row of ivory teeth. The growl rumbled on until Ned reared high, tumbling Natty into the magic wind so that she landed her proper size with a mighty bump. Pom Pom yelped with surprise and ran under the table to hide.

"Good gracious, Natty. What are you doing down there?" Mrs Potter demanded. "And what do you know about this mess in the hall?"

Sitting on the floor, Natty turned up frightened eyes.

"I … I…" Nothing would come out. She looked round for Ned.

"Goodness, Natty, don't tell me you're going to say there's a ghost in the house as well?" said Mrs Potter, clasping Natty's arm and hauling her up.

"There is a ghost," cried Natty, thinking this the best way to explain her confused state. "It's really freaky."

Mrs Potter brushed her down. From the corner of her eye Natty saw Ned gallop out of the back door. From under the table Pom Pom saw him too but having just missed being flattened he was staying put.

"It's all silly nonsense, Natty. I'm surprised at you," said Mrs Potter. "Pom Pom – what are you doing under the table? Naughty dog. Get in your bed." But Pom Pom wouldn't budge.

"I must go," said Natty, leaving Mrs Potter to pull the unwilling dog out. She darted into the utility room in time to see Ned leap into the garden and take cover behind a flowerpot. Natty breathed a sigh of relief and pulled on her wellies. Ned was safe.

Outside, Penelope and Trudi waited anxiously in the courtyard.

"Has the ghost gone?" called Penelope.

"We're not coming in until it has," said Trudi.

"Don't ask me," said Natty. "It might have. Then again it might still be lurking." Mrs Potter arrived at the doorstep and Natty made a run for it.

"Penelope, Trudi, come in at once. I suppose all this talk of a ghost in the house is an excuse for the disgraceful mess in the hall. I want it cleared up at once."

Natty hurried to escape, wondering how long it would take Mrs Potter to persuade them to go in and how long it would take Penelope and Trudi to clear up.

When she reached the gate at the bottom of the drive, Mr Potter drove in on his way back from the supermarket.

"Going already, Natty?" he said. "Here." And he reached over into a cool-bag. "Your Wally Whizzer. You can't go without that."

"Oh, thank you," said Natty. "Thanks very much."

With a wave Mr Potter drove on.

The gate to Penelope's stable-yard was open and a low whicker came from behind the hedge. Natty darted across the lane to find the big Ned hiding in the yard.

"Thank goodness you're safe. I thought Pom Pom was going to eat you."

"It would take more than a snappy poodle to do that," said Ned cheerily. "So that's a Wally Whizzer Wonderstick Ice-Cream, is it?"

"Yes, would you like some?" Natty asked, pulling off the wrapper which she scrunched into her pocket. "It's chocolate and ice-cream and has a fruity bit in the middle."

"Sounds delicious." Natty held it out and Ned bit off the end. "It is delicious."

When the Wally Whizzer was finished, Natty put the stick and the paper in the tack-room rubbish bin. When she returned, Ned was wearing his saddle and bridle.

"There's still time for a ride in Winchway Wood," he said.

"A ride," said Natty. "Yes, please!" She put her foot in the stirrup and sprang on to his back. Instantly she was dressed in the magic riding clothes, her perfect disguise. Natty shut the gate behind them and Ned trotted down the lane past Mrs Plumley's house and Natty's house and on towards the wood.

"A walk, a trot, a canter, a gallop, a leap or two over the fallen log and home again," said Ned, which is just what they did. Natty loved every moment of it, the trees rushing past as Ned galloped

up the path, the sense of togetherness as they jumped the log, and the sheer exhiliration of knowing how much better her riding had become since Ned had been teaching her. By the time they arrived back at the front gate, Natty was glowing with happiness.

"Thank you, Ned, that was a wonderful ride," she said.

"I'm glad you enjoyed it. And now it's time for me to return to my poster."

Her bedroom window was still open and Natty guessed which way Ned would go. The large leaves of the fig tree made the perfect staircase up to her windowsill. She slid to the ground, took a last look at her beloved magic riding clothes and let go of the reins.

Back in her jeans and sweatshirt, Natty watched the big Ned disappear and the tiny Ned trot round in front of her.

She bent down, held out flat palms, and
up he jumped. Pushing open the front
gate with her bottom, she carried
the tiny pony to the fig
tree and watched while
he leapt from leaf to
leaf all the way up
to her bedroom.
Then Natty hurried round the house to
the back door.

She found Dad in the kitchen, staring
at a piece of burnt toast in the toaster.
She pulled off her wellies.

"Still not working properly?"

"Not quite. Did you sort out Pebbles, and is Penelope better?"

"I did, and Penelope is better."

"Well done," said Dad, turning back to the toaster.

Natty hurried upstairs to her bedroom. Tabitha lay curled up on her bed and Ned gazed down from his poster. She wished the magic hadn't ended; now she would have to wait until next time.

She checked to see Pebbles grazing happily in his field on the other side of the lane and closed the window. Spinning round she dived on to her duvet.

"Tabs, guess what?" Tabitha woke up and stretched. "Ned's been a ghost. It was brilliant. And we had a fantastic ride in the woods. And something else, Penelope's got hundreds of rosettes on her wall." She looked up at the chestnut pony in the poster.

"Maybe one day I'll win a rosette. With a magic pony, anything can happen!"

The End